Text © 1988 Richard Edwards
Illustrations © 1993 Caroline Crossland
All rights reserved
First published in Great Britain 1993
by Julia MacRae
an imprint of Random House
20 Vauxhall Bridge Road, London SW1V 2SA

Random House Australia (Pty) Ltd
20 Alfred Street, Milsons Point, Sydney, NSW 2061

Random House New Zealand Ltd
18 Poland Road, Glenfield, Auckland, New Zealand

Random House South Africa (Pty) Ltd
PO Box 337, Bergvlei, 2012, South Africa

Printed in China

British Library Cataloguing-in-Publication Data
A catalogue record for this book is
available from the British Library.

ISBN 1-85681-137-9

TEN TALL OAKTREES

Richard Edwards

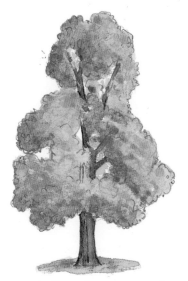

with pictures by

Caroline Crossland

Julia MacRae Books

LONDON SYDNEY AUCKLAND JOHANNESBURG

Ten tall oaktrees
Standing in a line,
"Warships," cried King Henry,
Then there were nine.

Nine tall oaktrees
Growing strong and straight,
"Charcoal," breathed the furnace,
Then there were eight.

Eight tall oaktrees,
Reaching towards heaven,
"Sizzle," spoke the lightning,
Then there were seven.

Seven tall oaktrees,
Branches, leaves and sticks,
"Firewood," smiled the merchant,
Then there were six.

Six tall oaktrees
Glad to be alive,
"Barrels," boomed the brewery,
Then there were five.

Five tall oaktrees,
Suddenly a roar,
"Gangway," screamed the west wind,
Then there were four.

Four tall oaktrees
Sighing like the sea,
"Floorboards," beamed the builder,
Then there were three.

Three tall oaktrees
Groaning as trees do,
"Unsafe," claimed the council,
Then there were two.

Two tall oaktrees
Spreading in the sun,
"Progress," snarled the by-pass,
Then there was one.

One tall oaktree
Wishing it could run,
"Nuisance," grumped the farmer,
Then there were none.

No tall oaktrees,
Search the fields in vain,
Only empty skylines
And the cold grey rain.